I0659185

the Eternal Journey

Gary J. Robbins

Editing, design, typesetting and publishing by UK Book Publishing

www.ukbookpublishing.com

ISBN: 978-1-917329-67-5

the Eternal Journey

"The eternal journey is one woven from hardship and grace, hope and joy, struggle and triumph — everything that makes life worth living. Through time, we are called to embrace every emotion, every fear, knowing that these experiences are part of a greater design, binding us together. There is no true end; it is an endless path, carrying us forward, pushing us to understand and grow.

In this journey, as we connect more deeply with each other and with ourselves, our capacity for love expands. The more we understand, the more we evolve, and the more we recognize the potential for greatness within us all. We are threads in the woven web of eternity, each of us contributing to the beauty and strength of the whole, united by the universal bond that draws us closer with each step.

Our lives are an expression of this truth, an ongoing story that will continue long after us, endlessly creating, endlessly loving."

— Gary J. Robbins

Dedication

To my brother, *Steve John Byrne* – my hero, my strength, the one I always looked up to. I hope you're in a better place, wherever you may be. Though this, my story *A Brother's Loss*, is woven from imagination, you were the real embodiment of resilience and bravery, and it's your battle, your strength, that inspired this book. Even in your fight against cancer, you taught me the power of courage and love.

To my friends and family, whose unwavering support and love have been a guiding light. For every hardship we've faced together, every moment we've learned and grown, and every time we've risen above – it's for you.

And to everyone who has ever lost a loved one and found themselves wandering in the shadows of grief, may this story offer you a glimmer of light in the darkness. In times of despair, remember that hope is all we need. This book is for you.

Prologue

THE MIRROR WITHIN

It began, as all things do, in silence.

In the quiet depths of my soul, long before I understood what it meant to truly see myself, there was an awareness – a presence waiting to be recognized. I had been so many things, worn so many faces, traversed so many paths, that the core of me seemed buried under layers of history and memory. And yet, here in this silence, there was a part of me that had never changed, a self untouched by time or experience, a light shining softly within.

As I gazed inward, I saw it – a reflection that wasn't defined by any single lifetime or identity. It was a vast, boundless self, shimmering like a mirror within, untouched by the wounds or triumphs of the lives I had lived. The mirror showed me not as I had been, not as I would be, but as I was – a soul stripped bare of title and story.

I found myself staring at the reflection, a quiet question forming in my mind: Who am I, beyond all I've known?

In that moment, every mask I had worn – the warrior, the father, the healer, the destroyer – fell away. Every story I had carried, every role I had embodied, dissolved like mist in the morning sun. And there, in the stillness, was simply me, the self that had been there through every twist and turn, every joy and sorrow, every birth and death.

In the mirror of my soul, I saw my essence as a pure light, neither wholly good nor evil, neither broken nor whole, but simply present. This light was soft, warm, radiating not with power or grandeur but with an unyielding gentleness. It was the light of acceptance, of beingness itself.

Yet as I continued to look, I saw more. The light shifted, revealing shadows – shadows I had tried to outrun across lifetimes. There was my anger, raw and unfiltered, a fierce storm raging within me. There was my grief, heavy as the depths of the sea, carrying the memories of every loved one I had lost. And there was my fear, a primal instinct that whispered of loss, of betrayal, of being forgotten.

For a moment, I wanted to turn away. I wanted to retreat from these shadows, from the pain that had woven itself into my very essence. But the mirror wouldn't allow it. It held me there, showing me every part of myself without judgment or pity.

Face it, the silence seemed to say. Face all of it.

And so I did. I allowed myself to feel the rage, the sorrow, the regret, and the fear – all the emotions I had tried so hard to push aside, to deny. I let them wash over me like a flood, their intensity raw and unyielding. I felt the anger of betrayal, the bitterness of defeat, the ache of countless goodbyes. I let myself feel it all, not as separate lifetimes but as one continuous current flowing through me.

And in feeling it, something changed. The shadows that had once seemed so vast, so insurmountable, began to soften, to blend into the light. They weren't separate from me. They were me – parts of myself that I had never fully embraced.

I began to understand that each shadow was not a flaw or a failing, but a piece of my journey, a lesson I had yet to integrate. My anger was the fire that had driven me to protect those I loved. My sorrow was the depth that had allowed me to feel compassion. My fear was the instinct that had kept me alive, guiding me through lifetimes of struggle.

In the mirror, the light and the shadows swirled together, merging into a single, unified whole. I was not one or the other; I was both. I was the light that yearned to create, to love, to uplift – and I was the shadow that had stumbled, that had made mistakes, that had hurt and been hurt.

As I continued to gaze, a new realization dawned: I was never broken. I was never incomplete. The pieces of myself that I had viewed as wounds or weaknesses were simply facets of a greater whole. My journey had been not to become perfect, but to become real – to understand that all of it, every part, was necessary.

The mirror's reflection shifted, and I saw myself not as a fractured being, but as a tapestry woven from countless threads, each one vibrant, essential. I was no longer Tristan the wanderer, Tristan the seeker, Tristan the flawed. I was simply Tristan, whole and unbroken, a soul made complete by the fullness of my journey.

I felt a profound peace settle over me, a quiet joy that needed no words. In that moment, I was free – not because I had erased my shadows, but because I had embraced them. I was free to be, free to love, free to continue my journey without the weight of past regrets or future fears.

The mirror began to fade, but its truth lingered within me, a guiding light that would carry me forward. I understood now that the journey would never end – that there would always be new shadows, new lessons, new lives to live. But I no longer feared them. I welcomed them, knowing that each one would add to the richness of who I was, of who I would become.

As I stepped away from the mirror, I felt lighter, clearer, more alive. I was no longer searching for answers, because I had found the only truth that mattered: I was whole, and I always had been. And wherever the journey led next, I would face it with open arms, knowing that each step, each breath, was part of the eternal dance that was life itself.

And so I walked forward, unafraid, ready to continue the journey, not as a man seeking completion, but as a soul who had finally found it.

Chapter 1

THE FIRST AWAKENING

There was no light, no sound, only the deep, enveloping stillness of the void. Consciousness stirred within the abyss, flickering like a small flame caught in the winds of eternity. It was not the heaven people imagined – a paradise awaiting the good – but a promise of something more. A promise that Heaven could only be reached through understanding, experience, and transformation.

I was not yet ready to transcend. I was incomplete, a mere fragment of what I would need to become.

But in the stillness, something began to shift. A soft warmth crept into the darkness, a sensation that reached beyond thought or form. I was becoming aware – not of myself, but of the pull, subtle yet undeniable, that had always been there. There was a sense of movement, of inevitability, as if I had always been on this path, though I had never known it.

There was no sound. Not yet. But the silence began to hum with potential, vibrating with the unspoken truths that lay on the other side. And in that hum, I began to see. Not with eyes, but with something deeper – an inner vision that opened as slowly and tenderly as a bloom in spring.

I had no name, no face, no identity. I was not a person, not yet. I was a consciousness, undefined and unshaped. But I was also a part of something much larger, something vast and incomprehensible. The void I floated in wasn't empty; it was filled with the energy of everything that ever was and ever would be.

A voice, not my own, seemed to stir within me. It is time.

There was no urgency, only an invitation. I felt the gentle tug – a pull toward life, toward becoming something more than I was. The darkness around me began to soften, and I sensed the presence of something beyond, something waiting just beyond the veil.

I was being given a chance. Not a gift, but a responsibility. Each life would be a new chance, a new lesson, a step toward completion. I could not ascend until I had lived through it all – every joy, every sorrow, every love, every loss. The journey would be long, and I would have to be reborn many times, but each rebirth was a step closer to understanding.

In that moment, I felt both the weight of eternity and the promise of freedom.

"Why?" The question sits heavy within me, like a stone sinking into the vastness of my own silence. This journey – I am bound to it, but I do not yet understand why. Why must I walk through these echoes of suffering and joy that are not my own? Why does each moment of warmth seem to pass just as I begin to feel it, leaving a cold emptiness in its place? I watch, I listen, I learn, but to what end?

Each glimpse of life leaves a shadow in me. The joys are fleeting, but the pain… it lingers, as if woven into my own spirit. When I see a mother lose her child, or a man sacrifice all he is for those he loves, I cannot help but feel as though I am there, as if their grief and hope are a mirror into something I am supposed to find within myself. But what am I supposed to see?

There are moments when I feel close, like a whisper brushing against my mind, telling me there is purpose here. But then it fades, leaving only questions in its wake.

Perhaps I must endure this to learn compassion – not the fleeting kindness of sympathy, but a depth of understanding that requires I stand in the fires of loss, of love, of sacrifice. I sense that these experiences will shape me, change me, but I wonder at the cost. How many lives must I pass through before I understand? And what will be left of me when I do?

There is a haunting ache within me, a weight of unspoken truths I am not yet ready to face. But I must press on, for if I turn away now, I will carry this same emptiness into whatever comes next. So, I ask again: why must I go through this? And when will I know that I have truly learned?

The first stirrings of light appeared at the edges of my awareness, not sharp but soft, like the first rays of a sun breaking through a distant horizon. With it came sound – not the harsh clamour of the world, but a gentle vibration, like a heartbeat, constant and reassuring.

I felt myself being drawn toward it. A presence enveloped me, not with hands but with intention, guiding me toward what was to come. I was falling – not in the way a body falls through space, but in the way a raindrop falls into the ocean, becoming part of something immeasurably larger than itself.

And with that fall, came a sense of acceptance. I was leaving behind the void, the nothingness, and stepping into the world of becoming. I would live, I would love, I would suffer, and I would learn. It was not a choice – it was a promise.

I began to descend, faster now, as if the pull had become an irresistible current. I did not resist; I couldn't. The light grew brighter, the sounds louder, and as I plummeted toward my first life, a single thought echoed in the recesses of my mind:

This is only the beginning.

And with that, I was born.

Chapter 2

LIFE THROUGH ANOTHER'S EYES

W hen I awoke again, I wasn't reborn in the way I expected. My form was different – not human, not flesh. I was a presence, an essence that lingered in the minds and hearts of others, a spiritual guide. I had no body of my own, no voice of my own. Instead, I drifted through the lives of those who would shape history, tethered to their thoughts, their doubts, and their hopes.

I became a whisper of courage in their darkest moments, the gentle nudge when they were poised to falter. I could not act, could not intervene in their choices, but I was there in the quiet spaces between, watching their souls twist with uncertainty, offering guidance they would never know came from me.

At first, this existence felt like freedom. There was something exhilarating about witnessing greatness unfold. I moved through time and space, seeing the rise of heroes, warriors, visionaries. I was there when their minds wavered, when their hearts raced with fear. I saw their struggles, their moments of indecision. But I also witnessed their triumphs, their victories, their glory.

It was easy to be consumed by it. These people – the ones I guided – they shaped the course of the world. Through their hands, empires rose and fell, art flourished, knowledge spread like wildfire. They were the makers of history, and I was there, silently entwined with their legacies.

But there was another side to it. With greatness always came sacrifice. The more I watched, the more I saw that every triumph came at a cost. The heroes I inhabited faced impossible choices – between love and duty, between personal happiness and the greater good. They gave their lives to causes larger than themselves, and in doing so, they lost something deeply human.

I felt their pain as if it were my own. Their burdens became mine. I learned that to be great often meant to endure heartache unimaginable to those who lived simpler lives. They loved deeply, but that love was always shadowed by the fear of losing what they held dear. They sacrificed personal joy for the sake of others, for the sake of something they believed in, but it broke them in ways they could not foresee.

In one life, I walked alongside a ruler whose decisions would change the fate of nations.

He had everything a man could desire – power, wealth, admiration. His throne stood atop a mountain of victories, each battle a testament to his strategic genius and unyielding will. His name was whispered in awe throughout the lands, his face immortalized in the finest sculptures, and his rule seemed destined to endure for centuries. Yet, beneath the crown of laurels and golden robes, he carried a weight that no riches or adulation could lift.

At night, when the court was silent and his armies rested, I would sit with him, though he could not see me. He sat alone on his grand balcony, gazing out over his kingdom, the very empire he had built with blood and steel. The air was thick with the scent of jasmine, and the stars hung low, but none of it brought him peace. His mind was a battlefield of its own, and I could feel the ghosts of those he had ordered into death circling him like a storm. Each victory, each city conquered, came at a cost, and though he had never held the sword himself, the blood was on his hands.

He had started with noble intentions – he truly believed that uniting the fractured lands under one rule would bring peace, that his wars were necessary to stop greater suffering. And in the beginning, the people revered him as a liberator. They threw flowers at his feet and sang songs of his greatness. But the flowers wilted, and the songs faded. As his power grew, so too did his hunger for more. He convinced himself that his reign was for the greater good, that the sacrifices he demanded were justified by the utopia he envisioned.

But the weight of those sacrifices was unbearable. Every soldier who fell on the battlefield, every child orphaned, every village razed to ash – these were not just casualties of war. They were lives, countless lives, shattered by his ambitions. At first, he pushed the grief away, burying it beneath the justification that this was the price of progress. But as the years passed, it festered like an infection, eating away at him from within.

I watched as the people around him changed. His trusted advisors grew distant, their voices tinged with doubt. His closest friends became silent, wary of the ruler he had become. Even his family, the wife who once adored him, the children who had looked up to him with wide, admiring eyes, now kept their distance, afraid of the man who could order thousands to their deaths without a second thought. His throne became a cage, each jewel in his crown a reminder of the lives he had destroyed to keep it.

One night, he stood on the edge of his balcony, staring down at the city below, now cloaked in darkness. He spoke aloud, though there was no one to hear him but me. "For the greater good," he whispered, as if trying to convince himself once more. His voice trembled. "It was for the greater good…" But the words felt hollow, even to him.

In that moment, I felt the full weight of his sorrow. His victories had cost him his soul. He had everything – power, wealth, admiration – but he had lost the very thing that made life worth living. He no longer saw the world through the eyes of a ruler, but through the veil of his own grief. His victories were nothing more than ashes in his hands, and the empire he had built was an empty monument to his regret.

In another life, I was a silent companion to a healer.

She was not born into greatness. She did not wear a crown or command armies. Her hands were worn and calloused from years of labour, her face marked by the lines of sleepless nights spent by the bedside of the dying. But she possessed a heart that burned with a fierce, unwavering love for humanity, a compassion so deep it bordered on self-destruction.

I followed her through the dimly lit halls of makeshift hospitals, where the air was thick with the scent of sickness and despair. She moved tirelessly from bed to bed, her hands soothing the fevered foreheads of the afflicted, her voice a soft murmur of comfort in the chaos. There was a kindness in her touch, a tenderness that seemed to ease the pain of those who suffered, even if she could not save them.

But for every life she healed, there were ten more she could not. She lived in a time of great plague, where death swept through villages like wildfire, leaving devastation in its wake. And though she fought valiantly against the tide of sickness, there were days when it seemed as if the more she healed, the more there was to heal.

I watched as she sat by the bedside of a young girl, no more than seven, her skin pale and clammy, her breathing shallow. The healer held her hand, whispering words of comfort as the girl's mother wept quietly in the corner. I could feel the strain in the healer's heart, the desperation as she tried everything she knew, every remedy she had learned, to pull the child back from the brink. But it was not enough. The girl slipped away in the night, her small hand limp in the healer's grasp.

The next morning, the healer's hands trembled as she wrapped the child's body in a linen shroud. Her eyes, once bright with determination, were now clouded with a grief so deep it seemed to consume her. I could feel the weight of every life she had lost pressing down on her, crushing her beneath a tide of guilt. She had poured every ounce of her energy, every fragment of her soul, into saving lives, but it was never enough. The ones she couldn't save haunted her, their faces etched into her memory, a constant reminder of her limitations.

I followed her as she retreated to a small, dimly lit room at the end of the day, her hands stained with blood and her spirit heavy with sorrow. She fell to her knees, her body shaking with silent sobs, and I could feel the depth of her despair. She had dedicated her life to healing, to mending the broken, but the endless cycle of death had become too much.

Her compassion, once her greatest strength, had become her curse. The more she loved, the more she suffered. She could not separate herself from the pain of those she tried to save, and it was slowly destroying her. Each life lost felt like a personal failure, each death a wound on her own soul.

In the quiet moments, when no one was watching, I could feel her doubt creeping in. Had she done enough? Could she have saved more? Was she really making a difference, or was she just prolonging the inevitable? These questions tormented her, gnawing at her spirit, until all that was left was a shell of the woman she had once been.

And yet, despite the crushing weight of her grief, she continued. Every morning, she rose before dawn, her body aching, her heart heavy, and she returned to the sick, the dying, the broken. Because deep down, she knew that even if she couldn't save them all, the ones she could save mattered. Every life, every person who walked away from her care healed, was worth the pain.

But the cost of that choice – the cost of her compassion – was her own soul. She had given everything, and in the end, there was nothing left for herself. She was a healer, yes, but the one person she could not heal was herself.

And yet, I couldn't intervene. I was there, guiding, whispering, but never able to change the course of events. I had to watch as these souls – these extraordinary people – made their choices, felt their pain, and bore the consequences of their decisions. It was their journey, and I was just a presence in the shadows.

Through them, I learned that greatness is not free. It demands everything, and more. The sacrifices are not only physical, but emotional, spiritual. It became clear that in order to guide others, I had to feel their suffering too. It was no longer enough to watch from a distance. I had to understand the cost of being human, of making impossible choices, of living with the weight of those choices.

This existence, though different, taught me that every soul is tested. Greatness is not just in the victories, but in the ability to endure the sacrifices that come with it. Every person I guided carried their own burdens, and though I was there to help them rise, it was their pain that truly shaped them – and me.

I am beginning to see lives not just as experiences but as layers – each one built upon the other, each shaping the next in ways I cannot fully understand. I entered their lives with curiosity, yet the moments of their greatest joy and darkest despair settle in me like a ghost that refuses to leave. In every sacrifice, I see an echo of my own, though I do not know what I've given, or why.

As I witness these souls forging their paths – leaders giving up peace for power, mothers giving up freedom for love – an unrelenting question arises within me: what am I meant to gain from their pain? With each choice they make, I feel something in myself respond, but it is like hearing a song from a distance, its meaning lost in the echo. There is a cost to greatness, that much is clear. But what cost am I paying, and for what?

I sense I am learning, but the lessons are fragmented. Each act of courage or despair reveals some part of the human soul, but I cannot piece them together. How many lives must I witness before the whole truth becomes clear? I have glimpses of understanding – a flash of empathy, a resonance of longing – but as soon as I reach for it, it dissolves, leaving only confusion. I press on, even as the weight of these lives settles into my spirit. But for how long can one walk in shadows without being consumed?

I am left asking, still, why? Why must I suffer alongside these souls, feeling the weight of lives that aren't my own? Why am I being shown this, and to what end? There is some purpose in it, some deeper meaning that I must unravel. But for now, I am left with only fragments, with pieces of a puzzle whose full picture eludes me.

Chapter 3

THE WEB OF LIFE

There comes a moment in every journey where the path opens up before you, and the magnitude of it all becomes clear. For me, that moment came as I stood at the crossroads of countless lives, each thread intertwined, stretching far beyond what I had once understood. It wasn't a grand revelation at first – just a feeling, like the gentle tug of a string I hadn't known was there. But as I followed it, tracing its connections, I began to see the intricate, fragile web that held everything together.

We like to believe that our actions are our own, that we walk through this world as individuals, carving our paths, making choices based on who we are in that moment. But the truth is far more complex. Every decision we make ripples outward, touching lives we may never even know, shifting the course of history in ways that are imperceptible at first but monumental in the grander scheme of things.

It began with a memory, of a guide to a warrior. His choices were driven by honour and duty, bound by the loyalty he held for his kingdom. On the surface, it seemed as though his life was his own, his choices born from the immediacy of battle and the survival of his people. But as I traced his steps through time, I saw something I hadn't realized before.

His decision to march into battle, to strike down his enemies, was not just about survival – it was a thread pulled tight by the hands of those who had come before him. The war he fought had begun generations earlier, a conflict sparked by a forgotten betrayal, a choice made in the heat of passion. It wasn't just about him – it was about the ruler who had once chosen greed over peace, about the healer who couldn't save a child. Their lives were all woven together, their stories connected by choices they didn't even know they were making.

This is the web of life. It stretches across time, across generations, and across every living being on this earth. Every action, no matter how small, sends ripples through it, touching the lives of others in ways we can't always see. It's easy to think that what we do in our short time here doesn't matter, that we are insignificant in the face of the vastness of the universe. But the truth is, we are all connected, bound by invisible threads that tie us to one another, to the earth, and to something far greater than ourselves.

The realization hit me with a force that was both humbling and overwhelming. I saw how one person's pain could echo through the lives of those around them, how one act of kindness could spark a change that might alter the course of history. I saw how wars were started, not by one man's decision, but by the accumulation of countless moments – fear, pride, greed – all building up until the scales tipped and the world was forever changed. I saw how love, in its purest form, could transcend lifetimes, binding souls together in ways that even death couldn't break.

I began to understand that nothing happens in isolation. The choices we make are never just about us – they are about everyone we touch, everyone who will come after us. The warrior who chose to fight didn't know that his decision would lead to the fall of a kingdom centuries later. The healer who saved a life didn't know that the child she spared would one day grow up to start a revolution, changing the course of a thousand lives.

This realization brought me a sense of both responsibility and awe. How could it be that we are so powerful and yet so blind to the impact we have? How could it be that every moment, every decision, was part of something so much larger, something that spanned time and space in ways we could never fully comprehend?

But it wasn't just the grand, life-changing decisions that shaped the web. It was the small moments, the ones we often overlook. A smile shared between strangers, a word of encouragement to someone in pain, the act of forgiveness when everything inside you tells you to hold onto anger. These moments are just as vital, just as powerful. They weave their own delicate threads into the tapestry of life, creating connections that ripple outwards, sometimes in ways we will never see.

I saw it clearly then – how humanity is like a vast, interconnected system, each of us a single node in the web. And with that clarity came the understanding of why we suffer, why we love, why we are compelled to seek meaning in this world. It is because we are not meant to live in isolation. We are meant to be part of something greater than ourselves.

In that moment, I realized that the web of life wasn't just about survival or the perpetuation of existence. It was about learning. Every experience, every joy, every heartbreak was a lesson, not just for the individual, but for all of us. We grow because we are connected, because we share in each other's pain and triumphs. We learn from the past, even if we don't realize it, and our choices shape the future in ways we may never understand.

And so, I found purpose. I wasn't just wandering through lives to observe, to be a passive participant in the stories of others. I was part of the web, a thread among countless others, connected to every soul that had come before and every soul that would come after. My choices mattered – not just for me, but for the world. It wasn't about finding the right path, but about understanding that every path, every choice, every moment, was part of the same tapestry.

There is something profoundly beautiful in that realization. It strips away the illusion of separateness, the idea that we are alone in our struggles. We are all walking the same path, even if we are on different journeys. And the love we share, the compassion we offer, the kindness we show, they all become part of the web, strengthening the bonds between us and making the world just a little bit brighter.

The web of life is fragile, yes, but it is also resilient. It can stretch and bend, but it doesn't break easily. And through it, we find connection, not just to each other, but to the earth, to the universe, to the very essence of existence. Every breath we take is part of a larger rhythm, every heartbeat a note in the symphony of life.

And then, just when I thought I had understood the full weight of this realization, I felt it – the tug of something deeper, something personal.

In the end, I wasn't ready to move on. I could feel it deep within me. I hadn't learned all there was to learn. The journey was far from over. I needed to experience more, to live through another's eyes in a way that brought me even closer to understanding the human condition. For now, I remained a guide, caught between the triumphs and tragedies of others, learning with each step what it meant to truly live, and to sacrifice.

Through all these lives, I felt their joys and sorrows, their love and loss, but I never truly lived. I was always separate, detached, floating above their reality like a distant observer. And then, without warning, something shifted.

It began as a flicker, a sensation I couldn't quite place. I had never felt it before – something that wasn't part of the ebb and flow of time. It grew stronger, pulling me from the endless cycle of witnessing others' lives into something different, something tangible. Slowly, I became aware of a body – not just the vague sense of form I had experienced before, but a real, living body, with all its fragility and wonder.

I felt warmth first, the heat of the sun on my skin, and it was intoxicating. My chest rose and fell with breath, each inhale filling me with a sense of presence I had never known. My heart was beating in steady rhythm, and with it came a rush of awareness – of what it meant to be human. It was terrifying and beautiful all at once. I was alive.

Every sensation was new. The sharpness of the air, the texture of the ground beneath my feet, the sound of my own voice as I tested words for the first time – it was overwhelming. I stumbled through those first days, like a newborn creature trying to make sense of the world around me. I had lived countless lives through the eyes of others, but nothing had prepared me for the visceral reality of living in my own skin.

There was fear, too – fear of this body that could be hurt, fear of the emotions that surged through me in ways I had never experienced before. Joy, sadness, anger, love – they all hit me with a force I hadn't expected. For so long, I had been a witness to these feelings, but now they were my own, and I wasn't sure how to contain them. Yet, even in the chaos of it all, there was a deep sense of awe. I had become something new, something whole.

It was in this rebirth that I began to understand what it truly meant to live. To be human was to be vulnerable, to feel both the wonder and the pain of existence. But it was also to be connected – to the earth, to others, to the very fabric of life. I could feel it now, coursing through me, like a river that had been waiting for me to dive in. And with it came a question I hadn't asked before: What did I want from this life?

I had no answer then, only the certainty that I was meant to find one. And in time, I did.

Chapter 4

A SIMPLE YET MEANINGFUL LIFE

I was born into the simplest of existences: that of a farmer. My hands were not the hands of a visionary or a warrior – they were rough, calloused, and worn by the soil. I had no grand destiny, no prophecy or higher calling. I was just a man, living in a small village where the land was my world, and the seasons dictated the rhythm of life.

It was a life of repetition. Each morning, I woke with the dawn, my body aching from the day before. I ploughed fields, planted seeds, tended to the animals, and harvested crops when the time came. There were no riches in this life, no fame, no glory. My joy came from watching the crops grow, from seeing the fruit of my labour slowly come to life. The rewards were small – a bountiful harvest, a healthy herd, a warm meal shared with my family at the end of the day – but they were everything to me.

At first, I didn't understand the purpose of this life. It felt insignificant compared to some of the lives I had lived before. I had been kings and scholars, lovers and revolutionaries, yet here I was, toiling away in the dirt, year after year. But as time passed, I began to see the quiet beauty in it. The land didn't demand greatness from me; it only asked for my care, my patience, my resilience. It gave me back just enough to keep going, to keep me grounded.

In that simplicity, I began to learn something I had never truly understood in all my previous lifetimes: contentment. There was a peace in the predictability, in the rhythm of nature. The sun would rise, and the crops would grow if I did my part. Life was harsh sometimes – the crops would fail, droughts would come, and livestock would die – but there was always the next season, always another chance to try again. Hope, in its most elemental form, lived here in the soil.

The land had always been our anchor. It was where Lydia and I first laid the foundation for our family and our future. She was more than just a partner; she was my heart, my strength, the one who made the harshness of life on the farm bearable. Lydia had a quiet, determined grace about her. Her beauty wasn't the kind that caught attention in a crowd, but the kind that stayed with you – the kind that lingered in the way she smiled after a long day, or how her laughter echoed in the open fields when the children played around us.

We met when we were young, and from the start, I knew she was unlike anyone I'd ever known. She could milk a cow before sunrise, stitch a tear in a shirt in a few minutes, and still find time to comfort our children when they woke with bad dreams. Her hands were always busy, always creating, fixing, nurturing. There was a sense of purpose in everything she did, and it spilled over into our life together. She believed in the land, in the life we were building, and in the family we were raising. Lydia was my foundation, and in her, I found the courage to keep going even on the hardest days.

We had four children – three boys and a girl – and each of them was a gift. Our eldest, Thomas, had Lydia's quiet determination. Even as a child, he worked alongside me, eager to learn the ways of the farm. Then there was Samuel, who was always full of energy, a dreamer at heart, with his head in the clouds. Sarah, our only daughter, had Lydia's kindness and warmth. She spent hours by her mother's side, learning how to bake bread and tend to the garden. Our youngest, Jacob, was still just a boy, full of life and mischief, always trailing behind his older siblings, trying to keep up.

Our days were long, but filled with the kind of contentment that comes from shared purpose. The children grew up in the rhythms of the farm, with the seasons marking the passage of time. Spring brought the planting, summer the hard labour under the hot sun, autumn the harvest, and winter the quiet waiting for the earth to renew itself. In those years, life was simple, and we found joy in the small things — the laughter of our children as they ran through the fields, the warmth of a fire on cold winter nights, the smell of fresh bread that filled our home.

But life, as I would come to learn in every one of my incarnations, is fragile.

It started with a cough. Just a little tickle in Sarah's throat at first, nothing to worry about. But within days, it spread to Jacob and then to Lydia. The village doctor came and went, offering remedies that did little more than provide a false sense of hope. Within a week, our home was filled with the sound of their laboured breathing, the weight of their fevered bodies heavy on our hearts.

I remember sitting by Sarah's bedside, holding her small, pale hand as she drifted in and out of consciousness. She was so young, so full of life only days before, and now I could feel her slipping away from me. Lydia tried to stay strong for the children, but I saw the fear in her eyes — the fear that no parent should ever have to feel, the fear of losing what you love most.

One morning, after a night that seemed to stretch into eternity, Sarah's breathing grew shallow. I held her close, feeling her small body tremble in my arms. Her eyes fluttered open for a brief moment, and in that moment, she looked at me — not with fear, but with a quiet acceptance that shattered my heart.

"I love you, Papa," she whispered, her voice barely audible.

I held her tighter, but I knew it was too late. Her breath slowed, and then, it stopped. My little girl, my Sarah, was gone.

The grief hit me like a storm, but there was no time to process it. Jacob's condition worsened quickly after that. My youngest son, the boy who had always been full of life and mischief, grew quieter as the sickness took hold. Lydia stayed by his side, refusing to leave him even for a moment, but nothing we did could change the course of fate. Jacob, too, slipped away from us, leaving a silence in the house that was deafening.

The house that had once been filled with the sound of laughter, with the joy of children playing and the warmth of a family united, was now filled only with the echoes of what had been.

Lydia and I were left with Thomas and Samuel, but the loss of Sarah and Jacob weighed heavily on all of us. Lydia, who had always been the strongest among us, seemed to wither under the weight of her grief. She went through the motions – feeding the animals, tending to the farm – but the light in her eyes had dimmed. At night, I would find her sitting by the empty beds of our lost children, her hands resting on the blankets they had once slept under, her face drawn with sorrow.

There are no words to describe what it feels like to watch the person you love most in the world lose the will to live. Lydia was still there, physically, but I could feel her slipping away from me, just as surely as Sarah and Jacob had. I tried to comfort her, to remind her that we still had each other, that we still had Thomas and Samuel, but my words felt hollow. How do you tell someone to keep going when they've lost a part of themselves?

The winter that followed was the coldest I had ever known – not because of the weather, but because of the emptiness that filled our home. The loss of our children had left a wound that I wasn't sure would ever heal. Lydia's health declined as well, her body weakened by the grief that consumed her. One night, as I sat beside her, watching her pale face illuminated by the dim glow of the fire, she turned to me and said something I'll never forget.

"I'll see them again, won't I?" she asked, her voice barely a whisper.

I didn't have the heart to tell her that I didn't know. That after all the lives I had lived, I still didn't fully understand the mysteries of death and what came after. But I nodded and held her close, because in that moment, hope was all we had left.

Lydia passed away a few weeks later, leaving me alone in a house that now felt like a tomb. I buried her beside Sarah and Jacob, under the old oak tree that stood on the edge of our land. It was a cold, grey morning when I laid her to rest, the sky heavy with the promise of snow. Thomas and Samuel stood by my side, their faces pale, their eyes reflecting the same grief I felt.

In that moment, as I stood over the graves of my wife and children, I felt more alone than I ever had in any of my lifetimes. I had faced death before, had lost people I loved, but this... this was different. This was a kind of pain that no amount of experience could prepare you for. The loss of a child, the loss of a wife, the loss of a family – there are no words for that kind of grief. It is something that consumes you, that hollows you out from the inside, leaving you with nothing but an aching emptiness.

But even in the depths of that despair, there was something that kept me going. It was a quiet, almost imperceptible flicker of hope. The hope that Lydia had clung to in her final moments – the hope that somewhere, somehow, we would all be reunited again. That this life, with all its pain and suffering, was not the end.

It wasn't a hope I could fully understand, not yet. But it was enough to keep me moving forward, one day at a time. Because in the end, hope is all we have. Hope is what allows us to endure the unendurable, to keep going even when everything else has been taken from us.

And so, I did the only thing I knew how to do. I picked up my tools, went back to the fields, and continued to tend to the land. Because in the rhythm of the seasons, in the cycles of life and death, I found a kind of solace. Life would go on, even without the ones I loved. The land would continue to grow, and in its quiet persistence, it taught me that even in the face of loss, there is always the possibility of renewal.

As the years passed, Thomas and Samuel grew into men, strong and capable, carrying on the legacy of the farm. They married, had children of their own, and life, in its own way, continued. But I never forgot Lydia, or Sarah, or Jacob. Their absence was a part of me, a scar that I carried with me for the rest of my days. But that scar also reminded me of the love we had shared, the joy we had known, and the hope that one day, we would be together again.

I have walked the earth as a king, a soldier, a scholar – and yet, it was in this life, as a farmer, that I experienced the most profound depth of love and loss. How strange that in this life, with hands bound to the soil, I learned the meaning of devotion, of building a life from nothing, only to see it slowly slip from my grasp.

There is a quiet beauty to the rhythm of the land, to a life so firmly anchored in simplicity. Here, purpose is clear and measured: you plant, you nurture, you wait, and if you are fortunate, you reap what you have sown. But I am beginning to understand that the true harvest is not what we pull from the soil but what grows within us as we tend to what we love.

Lydia – my heart, my soul, my strength – how do I begin to comprehend her loss? How does one explain the feeling of watching the person who is your very foundation slip away, like the last light of day fading into darkness? She was everything I thought I understood about love, and yet her absence taught me something I had never known – that the deeper the love, the more unbearable its loss. And my children... God, my children. How can any heart endure watching the light fade from the eyes of one so young, so innocent?

The ache is unimaginable. In each shallow breath of Sarah, in Jacob's last, laboured exhale, I felt the world crack open beneath my feet. It is as if a part of my soul was torn from me, leaving a raw emptiness that nothing in this life could ever fill. I have known pain in other lives, but this... this was something that left me broken in a way I cannot heal.

Why, I ask myself, must I endure such suffering? What am I to learn from this agony that sears through every fibre of my being? There is no glory here, no redemption. Only a life returned to the soil, the relentless passage of seasons, the rising and setting of the sun that goes on, indifferent to the pain it illuminates.

I cling to Lydia's final words – "I'll see them again, won't I?" – and wonder if perhaps this grief, this unyielding sorrow, serves some purpose beyond my understanding. Is it hope that drives us to continue, to pick up the pieces and keep going, despite the void left behind by those we loved? Or is it merely survival, an instinct deeper than reason?

I am learning, slowly, that perhaps it is in the smallest moments of grace – the quiet hope that life will go on, that the earth will yield another harvest – that we find the strength to endure. Even as I hold this pain, there is a flicker of something I cannot quite name. It is not peace, for there is no peace in such loss. But perhaps, like the land itself, I must learn to accept the rhythm of things. Life and death, love and loss – they are the seasons we must all endure.

I am lost, floating between worlds, bound to this suffering yet beginning to see glimpses of something greater. In each life, I am beginning to understand that every joy comes with a price, and perhaps the lesson is not in avoiding the pain but in bearing it with the resilience of the earth beneath me.

This journey, I realize, has only just begun. As I am reborn once more, I carry the weight of my past, of every love and loss, into the unknown. I do not know what lies ahead, but if there is one truth I hold close, it is this: in the highest of joys and the deepest of sorrows, there is a thread that binds them together, a lesson woven into the fabric of life itself. And so I continue, one step at a time, hoping that in each incarnation, I come closer to the understanding that eludes me still.

Chapter 5

A BROTHER'S LOSS

In the turbulent shadow of a war-torn land, we were born. Three brothers, bound by blood, but perhaps more so by the trials we endured side by side. Our mother used to say we each carried the flame of our ancestors – a fire that grew fiercer with each generation, passed down like an unbreakable oath. But in times like these, that flame wasn't just a symbol of our heritage; it was a torch lighting the path to survival.

We were part of a fractured empire – an ancient realm once unified and powerful, now split by civil war. The old order crumbled, and with it, the codes of honour and the bonds of loyalty that once held men together. Factions rose and fell, leaders declared themselves kings, and warriors became little more than pawns in a deadly game of power. Battles waged not only in open fields but also in the quiet corners of our cities, between friends and brothers who once shared a drink, now aiming arrows at each other's hearts. For us, survival meant not only holding our own but protecting each other.

We didn't fight for glory or riches, nor for any cause but one another.

We were all young men, just trying to live in a world that had no place for us, no mercy for our youth or dreams. We weren't a polished unit, just three brothers with a fierce sense of loyalty. But loyalty alone didn't win battles – it was earned in the spaces between action and sacrifice, forged in sweat, blood, and shared fears.

The eldest was Lorcan, the warrior who would never turn down a fight. Tall, broad-shouldered, and seemingly carved from stone, he was the first to throw himself into the fray, carrying the weight of a thousand expectations. People looked up to him, as if he was a beacon in the darkness, a leader without a crown. He wore his scars like medals, each one a testament to battles fought and victories claimed. But those who knew him closely could see the burden that came with it, the weight of knowing that if he ever faltered, we would all fall with him.

Lorcan had a way of rallying us with his unshakeable courage. To him, each battle was not a mindless clash but a matter of honour and justice, even if it meant facing impossible odds. He taught us not to fight just to win, but to fight for something worth defending. Though he never said it outright, we knew we were his cause, the brothers he'd die to protect.

Then there was Calem, our middle brother. He was quieter than Lorcan, but his silence held a strength that was no less fierce. Calem was our heart, the one who could read our pain without a word spoken. Where Lorcan inspired us, Calem held us together. His empathy ran deeper than any blade could cut, and he fought not with rage but with an unwavering resolve that made him formidable.

Calem saw the suffering around us and let it fuel his compassion. He was the one who would treat a fallen enemy with the same respect as an ally, burying them with dignity, whispering words of peace as he laid them to rest. He told us that in war, it was easy to lose your humanity, to become a monster, and that we had to hold onto whatever light we had left. When Lorcan's wrath and my recklessness flared, Calem was the one who pulled us back from the edge.

And then there was me, the youngest, Tristan. I was the free spirit, the one who wore anger like armour. Where Lorcan charged forward and Calem held steady, I was the unpredictable one, the spark that could either ignite hope or burn everything around it. I had a rebellious streak, a need to push against the boundaries that my brothers respected. The world was unfair, brutal, and I didn't care for its rules. I fought to break free, even if I didn't fully know what I was fighting for.

I looked up to Lorcan, admired his strength, and loved Calem's calm wisdom, but I also felt my own path diverging. I knew I wasn't made for their kind of honour;

there was too much anger in me, anger at a world that had taken so much from us and demanded more. In our unity, I felt both a fierce loyalty and a yearning for something beyond this endless war. But I would die for them, no matter what path my heart whispered to me in secret. They were my tether to the world, the reason I stayed in the fight.

The empire, once a sprawling beacon of unity, had become a labyrinth of shifting alliances and relentless bloodshed. We were warriors by necessity, not by choice. For years, we fought in skirmishes across fractured territories, taking orders from commanders whose loyalty was as fleeting as the sunrise. Our enemy wasn't just the faction across the field; it was the very empire that once promised to protect its own. Betrayals became the currency of war, and trust was a luxury none of us could afford. Yet, we held on to each other.

In one of our last campaigns, we found ourselves fighting to protect a town – a mere speck in the empire's crumbling map, but a place that had once been our mother's home. There was no strategic value, no wealth, nothing that the warlords would want. But to us, it was sacred ground. The people there knew of us, knew our family's name, and they looked to us as their last line of defence. We weren't just fighting for survival now; we were fighting for a legacy, for the chance to keep something of our past alive.

Lorcan led our small unit, his voice a rallying cry that cut through the chaos. Calem tended to the wounded, his touch gentle even as death hovered close by. And I – my role was to guard the flank, to hold the line with every ounce of fury I had. As the enemy pressed forward, I felt my anger swell, a storm building inside me, fuelled by the fear of losing my brothers.

The cold dawn had broken as we stood on the outskirts of our homeland, the air thick with the smell of earth and iron. A line of darkened figures gathered in front of us, our final stand against an enemy with no face, no mercy. This was no grand battlefield – just a simple valley, with the rising sun casting pale light over the bodies of those who had fallen in the days before. In the distance, we could see our mother's town, the smoke from hearth fires, the last remnant of peace in a world that seemed to thrive on tearing families apart.

This was not the first time we had fought, but somehow, we knew it might be the last. I could feel it in Lorcan's stance, see it in the way Calem's hands shook for just a moment as he gripped his sword. And in me – a fury that roared to life, tempered only by the presence of my brothers beside me. We fought not just for survival, but for each other, for the memories we shared, for the hope that someday, somehow, the nightmare would end, and we'd walk away together.

Lorcan, ever our leader, took the first charge, his sword raised high as he barrelled forward with a battle cry that seemed to shake the earth. He was strength embodied, an unbreakable force that had guided us through every fight, every storm. Behind him, Calem and I followed, his calm shadow and my reckless flame. We had no chance of winning, not against these odds, but in that moment, it didn't matter.

The clash of steel and screams filled the air, and we became something other than men − we became wrath, loyalty, love − all of it entwined in every swing, every block. I felt my heart pounding in my chest, the familiar thrill of the fight mixed with a gnawing ache, the realization that this was it. This was where we would make our final stand, together.

Lorcan fought like a man possessed, his blows landing with the precision and power of someone who was more than just a warrior − he was a brother, fighting not for himself, but for us. His strikes were deadly, his face a mask of defiance, a wall of courage that dared anyone to challenge him. He held the line, protecting us as he always had, with a fierceness that was almost unearthly.

But even the strongest can be broken. I saw the glint of a blade as it arced toward him, and for a heart-stopping moment, everything seemed to slow. Lorcan's body staggered, a sword thrust deep into his side. His face twisted in pain, but he didn't cry out. Instead, he turned to look at us, a soft, almost apologetic smile breaking through his mask of defiance. He was saying goodbye, even if he didn't have the words. I reached out, wanting to call to him, to pull him back, but it was too late.

He fell to his knees, his hand clutching his side as blood seeped through his fingers. Even as his life faded, his gaze stayed fixed on us, unyielding, a final promise etched in the quiet strength of his eyes. My heart felt like it was shattering, breaking in ways I couldn't even comprehend. Lorcan, our pillar, our unbreakable leader – gone.

I barely had time to process Lorcan's fall before Calem surged forward, his face a mixture of grief and resolve. He didn't hesitate, his hand reaching out to touch Lorcan's shoulder, a last farewell, before he stepped in front of me, shielding me with his own body.

"Tristan," he murmured, glancing back at me, his face pale but calm. "Stay close."

His voice was a balm, a reassurance in the midst of chaos. Calem fought with a grace and resolve that was almost poetic, his every movement filled with purpose. He didn't rage or scream; he fought as he had lived, quietly, selflessly, a protector in every sense. But even he couldn't withstand the relentless assault.

An enemy blade found its way past his guard, slicing deep into his shoulder, and then another into his side. He stumbled, gasping as blood poured from his wounds, but he did not fall. With the last of his strength, he turned to face me, his eyes filled with love and sadness, as if he was apologizing for leaving me alone.

"Stay alive," he whispered, his voice barely audible over the sounds of battle. Then, with a final breath, he sank to his knees, his body crumpling beside Lorcan's.

I was alone, the last of us standing, and the world seemed to blur around me. My heart felt hollow, filled with a grief so sharp it was like a blade carving into my soul. Lorcan and Calem, my brothers, my family – gone, taken by a world that knew nothing of mercy. I wanted to scream, to rage, to tear everything apart, but all I could do was stare, the weight of their loss crushing me.

Then, something within me snapped. The grief twisted into rage, a fire so fierce it threatened to consume me. I surged forward, my vision red with fury, my only thought to make them pay, to fight until there was nothing left of me. I threw myself into the fray, each swing of my sword a tribute to my brothers, each enemy that fell a small, hollow victory.

I fought with the strength of all three of us, driven not by hope, but by pure, unbridled pain. My body was battered, my wounds many, but I didn't feel them. I was a storm, a force of vengeance, my brothers' faces etched into my mind, their voices echoing in my ears. I was no longer fighting for survival; I was fighting for them, for the love we had shared, for the promises we had made.

But even I could not hold forever. I felt the sting of a blade sink deep into my side, then another across my back. My strength began to wane, my vision blurred, but I kept going, kept fighting, until I could no longer stand. My legs gave way, and I fell to my knees, the world around me fading as I looked out over the battlefield, seeing only the faces of my brothers, their smiles, their laughter, the moments we had shared.

As I lay there, my life ebbing away, a strange peace settled over me. I felt Lorcan's strength, Calem's calm, their spirits lingering beside me as if to guide me into whatever lay beyond. I wasn't afraid. Somehow, I knew that this wasn't the end, that even though we had been torn apart in this life, something stronger than death bound us together.

In that quiet moment, I felt the bond between us, a thread that stretched across time and space, unbreakable, eternal. We would meet again; I was certain of it, even if I didn't know how or where. Maybe in another life, in another world, but we would find each other. The love we shared, the loyalty, it was too fierce, too deep to simply vanish. We were bound not just by blood, but by something beyond it, a connection that went beyond words, beyond life itself.

As my vision faded and the last of my breath escaped, I closed my eyes, a soft smile on my lips. Somewhere, somehow, I would see them again. This was not goodbye – only a pause, a chapter in a story that would never truly end.

In the silence of that final moment, I knew with absolute certainty: we would be together again, and our bond would carry on, beyond the reach of time and death.

Chapter 6

LOVE AND LOSS

And then I found her.

She had been through hell before I met her – her eyes carried the weight of it, the kind of heaviness that doesn't fade, even when masked by a smile. There was a haunted look in those deep brown eyes, like they had witnessed more than they could bear. They told stories her lips never spoke, each glance carrying an unspoken history of pain, betrayal, and fear. Life had dealt her a hard hand.

She wore it in the way she moved – cautious, as though each step could bring her back to the very precipice of that hell she'd crawled out from. I saw it in her trembling hands when she thought no one was looking, the way they shook just slightly as if they still carried the weight of burdens she couldn't put down. Loud noises would make her flinch, her body tensing as though bracing for an impact she had learned to expect. There were nights when she would wake from her sleep with a gasp, her breath ragged, as if she had

been running from something in her dreams that had
yet to let her go.

But perhaps the hardest part to witness was the
way she always waited for the ground beneath her
to crumble. There was a constant vigilance in her, a
readiness to lose everything at any moment. It was as
if she had made peace with the idea that nothing good
in her life would last, because nothing good had lasted
before. She had built walls, tall and thick, around her
heart, shielding herself from the world, from anyone
who might cause her more pain. It took time – so much
time – for me to even begin to scale those walls.

Yet, even in all that brokenness, there was a beauty in
her spirit. She didn't let the world break her completely,
though it had come close more times than she would
admit. There was a quiet strength in her, a resilience
that ran deep, as though every scar on her heart had
shaped her into something unyielding, something more
enduring than the pain she had suffered. She had
survived when most would have been crushed under
the weight of it.

There were moments, in the beginning, when
I caught glimpses of that strength. Small flashes of
defiance, like a flicker of light in the darkness. I saw it in
the way she would pull herself together after a bad day,
her chin lifting just slightly as if to challenge the world
to try again. I saw it in her stubborn refusal to give

up on even the smallest joys — like the way she'd hum softly to herself while tending to her garden, her fingers brushing over the petals of flowers as though they were precious treasures. Those moments seemed to remind her, even if only briefly, that not everything in life was about survival; some things were still worth savouring.

She had been hurt — deeply, irrevocably — but she had not become bitter. That was what drew me to her in the end. She had every reason to turn cold, to push everyone away, but she didn't. Beneath all the layers of hurt, there was a tenderness, a yearning for connection. It was as if, despite everything, she still wanted to believe in the possibility of love, though she could hardly admit it to herself. That yearning was fragile, buried beneath years of hurt, but it was there. I could feel it in the way she looked at me sometimes when she thought I wasn't paying attention, her gaze softening for just a moment before she quickly looked away, as if afraid to let herself hope.

And when she let me in — when she finally let down those walls, even just a little — I saw all the pieces of her heart that had been shattered. I held those pieces with care, knowing how fragile they were, knowing how long it had taken for her to trust anyone again. There were days when she would smile at me, and it was like watching the sun break through the clouds after a long storm. But there were also days when the darkness would creep back in, when her past would weigh too heavily on her, and she would retreat into herself, lost in memories of things she couldn't forget.

In those moments, all I could do was hold her, even when she resisted. I would wrap my arms around her trembling frame, feeling her body shake as she tried to hold back the tears, tried to pretend she was fine. She hated being seen as vulnerable – it reminded her too much of the times when she had been powerless. But I saw her vulnerability as a kind of strength, because it took courage for her to show even a fraction of what she had endured.

We didn't speak much about the past in detail, not at first. I think it was too painful for her to recall it, and I never wanted to push her into reliving those moments of trauma before she was ready. But slowly, over time, she shared bits and pieces with me. The things she had gone through were worse than I had imagined. She had loved someone once – a man who had broken her in ways that words couldn't fully capture. The violence, the manipulation, the isolation – he had taken her to the edge of herself, stripping away her sense of worth, leaving her to believe that she was nothing without him.

But she had left him. Somehow, despite the fear and the control he had exerted over her, she had found the strength to leave. That strength, I realized, had come at a cost. She had sacrificed parts of herself in order to survive, and though she had escaped physically, there were still pieces of her soul that were trapped in that place, with him. Every time she flinched at a loud noise, every time she pulled away from me when I tried to get too close, I knew those were the parts of her still bound to her past.

It wasn't easy for her to believe in love again. There were days when I thought she might never fully let herself trust me, when the scars of her past seemed too deep, too permanent. But slowly, day by day, she began to let me in. I could see it in the small things – the way she'd rest her head on my shoulder without tensing, the way she'd reach for my hand without hesitation. And in those moments, I knew that love wasn't just about romance or passion. It was about healing, about being there for someone even when they weren't sure they deserved it.

She had been through hell, but together, we found a way out. And in loving her, I realized that sometimes, the greatest strength comes from surviving the things that were meant to break you, and still being able to open your heart again, even if just a little. She didn't need to be saved – she had already saved herself – but together, we rebuilt the pieces that had been broken. She taught me that love is not always about grand gestures or fairy-tale endings. Sometimes, love is simply the quiet act of holding someone when they're too tired to hold themselves.

Her name was Annabella. From the first moment we spoke, it was as if the world had shifted, like the universe had conspired to bring us together in that instant. There was a connection, a pull between us, that went far deeper than attraction. It wasn't just love – it was something older, something unspoken and eternal, as though our souls had been waiting for this reunion through the ages. The way she looked at me, with eyes that seemed to recognize parts of me even I hadn't known, made me realize that our meeting wasn't by chance. It felt as if we had found each other again, after wandering through lifetimes lost and apart, and now, we were finally whole.

Annabella had that quiet power about her, the kind that can steady a man with a single touch. Her presence was like a balm for the wounds I carried, soothing the scars left by my past – the pain, the grief, the guilt that had shadowed me for so long. She never knew how much she healed me simply by being. She didn't need to. It was her nature, her very existence, that brought a sense of peace I hadn't thought possible. In her company, the burdens I carried seemed lighter, as though the weight of the world had shifted just enough for me to breathe again.

We built a life together, though it often felt like we were defying the odds, walking a tightrope between love and loss. Every moment with her felt fragile, like we were holding something so precious, so delicate, that it could shatter at any time. That awareness never left us; it lingered in the background of our days, reminding us of the fleeting nature of happiness, of how easily life could change. But instead of letting that fear distance us, it made our love more intense, more deliberate. We cherished each moment as if it could be our last. The fragility of what we had didn't make us afraid to hold on to it – it made us cling to each other more fiercely.

We poured ourselves into one another, like two weary souls seeking refuge in the only place they could truly feel at home. Annabella understood pain – she knew it intimately, the way only someone who had endured it could. She carried her own scars, her own silent grief, and yet she never let it define her. Instead, she rebuilt herself, piece by piece, stronger and more beautiful because of the struggles she had faced. In her arms, I found a comfort I had never known, a sanctuary where the pain of the past no longer had the power to consume me. And I like to think that she found the same in me – that, together, we created a space where we could heal, not only from our own battles but from the battles we fought for each other.

Our life wasn't extravagant, but it was ours. On most nights, we would sit on the porch long after the sun had set, the cool night air wrapping around us like a blanket. We would talk, sometimes for hours, about everything and nothing, our voices blending with the sound of the wind rustling through the trees. Sometimes we would fall into comfortable silence, letting the stillness between us speak more than words ever could. I would watch her as she gazed up at the stars, her face soft in the moonlight, and I would wonder how I had ever lived without her. In those quiet moments, it felt like the rest of the world had fallen away, leaving only us, suspended in time.

There was a kind of magic in those nights – an intimacy that went beyond words. We shared the deepest parts of ourselves, laying bare our fears, our dreams, and the shadows that still lingered from our pasts. Annabella never shied away from the darkness within her, nor did she try to hide it from me. She had learned, as I had, that real love wasn't about pretending the shadows didn't exist – it was about finding someone who could stand with you in the midst of them, who could see your darkness and still choose to stay. And that's what we did. We stood together, even when the past threatened to pull us under, even when the weight of our shared grief became too much to bear.

There were nights when the pain of our pasts seemed too close, when the memories we had tried so hard to bury came rushing back, threatening to overwhelm us. Annabella would tremble in my arms, and I would hold her, wishing I could take her pain away, knowing that I couldn't. In those moments, we didn't need to speak. We understood each other in a way that went beyond words. I knew her pain, because I had felt it too. I knew her fear, because it was mine as well. And though neither of us said it out loud, there was always an unspoken understanding between us – that life was fragile, that happiness was something we could never take for granted.

We lived with that awareness, every day. It was what made our love so powerful, so consuming. We knew that it could all be snatched away in an instant, that the peace we had found was something we had to hold on to with everything we had. But we didn't let that fear drive us apart. Instead, it brought us closer, made every moment with her feel like a gift. I loved her more deeply, more fiercely, because I knew how easily it could all disappear. And she loved me the same way.

We didn't need grand gestures or promises of forever. What we had was real, grounded in the understanding that forever wasn't guaranteed – that all we had, all we ever truly had, was each other, here and now. And in that truth, we found a love that was stronger than the fragility of life, stronger than the pain of the past. A love that would endure, even when everything else crumbled away.

When our son was born, I saw a side of Annabella I hadn't known existed. She glowed in a way that was almost ethereal, as if every hardship, every battle she had fought in life had led her to this single, perfect moment. It was as if all the pain and suffering she had endured were wiped away the moment Luca was placed in her arms. She held him with a tenderness that only a mother who had truly known loss could possess, and in that instant, it felt as if she had found the piece of herself she had been missing all along. Her eyes, always so full of history and shadows, now sparkled with a kind of hope I hadn't seen before.

Luca became the centre of our world, the bright light that illuminated all the dark corners we had once feared. His presence was a balm, not just for Annabella, but for me too. We were no longer just two souls finding solace in each other's brokenness; we were a family. Something neither of us had dared to dream of, yet something we had both longed for in different ways. The love Annabella and I shared only grew deeper, stronger, more unshakable. And Luca was the purest reflection of that love – a living embodiment of all the beauty we had fought so hard to reclaim in a world that could often seem so cruel and unforgiving.

For a time, it felt as though we had finally escaped the shadows that had once loomed so large over our lives. We laughed more – oh, how we laughed. Luca's joy was infectious, his laughter filling the spaces of our home that had once echoed with the weight of unspoken fears.

We held each other closer, as if the fragility we once feared had been replaced by something solid, something unbreakable. Life became about the small, beautiful moments we hadn't known how to cherish before – our son's first steps, the sound of his voice calling us, the way his tiny hand would curl around our fingers as if we were his whole world.

Annabella, for all her strength and resilience, was never the same after Luca. She softened, in the best way, her edges smoothed by the unconditional love she felt for our son. I would often find her sitting by Luca's crib, just watching him sleep, her fingers lightly brushing through his hair. And in those quiet moments, she would whisper, almost as if afraid to say it too loud, "I never thought I could have this." Her voice would tremble under the weight of her past, the scars she still carried, as if she couldn't quite believe this happiness was hers to keep.

Her words would cut through me every time. Because I understood. I understood the fear behind them, the knowledge that life had never been kind to people like us. We had known too much pain, too much loss, to ever fully trust that happiness could be permanent. But that was what made it all the more precious – the awareness that this love, this family we had built, was something we could lose, something we had to hold onto with everything we had.

I would wrap my arms around her then, holding her close as she sat by Luca's side, and whisper back, "We have this now. This is real." And in that moment, with our son between us, it felt like enough to banish the fears that still lingered at the edges of our hearts. We had found our light, our reason to keep fighting. And for as long as we had it, nothing else mattered.

But life, as always, had other plans.

The day it happened, I remember the sky painted in hues of orange and pink, casting a peaceful glow over the world. It felt like one of those rare moments when everything was right, when the chaos of life settled into a fleeting calm. Annabella walked beside me, her hand intertwined with mine, and Luca skipped ahead, laughing as he chased the last rays of the setting sun. There was no warning, no sign that the world was about to shatter.

We were nearing home when a cry for help pierced the stillness of the evening air. It was desperate, raw — a sound that reached into my soul. I felt the familiar surge of instinct, the same one that had guided me through countless moments before. I couldn't stand by and watch someone suffer. Annabella always said that was both my greatest strength and my deepest flaw — this unrelenting need to help others, even when it meant risking everything.

Without thinking, I ran toward the sound. My legs moved on their own, my mind focused only on the person in distress. Annabella shouted after me, her voice laced with panic, but I couldn't stop. There, in a narrow alleyway, I found a man being attacked. There was a struggle, a flurry of confusion and fear. I barely had time to react before the sharp, cold blade cut through the air and pierced my side. The pain was instant, like fire spreading through my veins, but the shock was worse. I stumbled backward, my hand instinctively reaching for the wound as warmth pooled beneath my fingers.

I collapsed to the ground, the world around me spinning. Through the haze of pain, I heard Annabella scream. I turned my head, and there she was, frozen in terror, her eyes wide with horror as she rushed toward me. I wanted to reach for her, to tell her everything would be okay, but the words wouldn't come. My breath grew shallow, my vision blurred, but I could still see the anguish on her face – the raw, unfiltered fear of a woman watching the man she loved slip away.

Time slowed. Each second stretched out like an eternity. I wasn't gone yet, but I could feel myself leaving. My body, heavy and numb, was giving in, but something deeper within me fought to stay. Not for my own sake – I had made peace with the idea of death long ago – but for Annabella. For Luca. They needed me. I couldn't leave them, not like this.

As I lay there, my vision fading to darkness, I realized that this wasn't the end – not for me, at least. I felt something hold me back, a force stronger than the pull of death. It wasn't that I was surviving; it was that I wasn't allowed to leave.

I stayed tethered to this world, trapped in a space between life and death. I could still see, still feel, still love – but I was powerless to do anything. I watched as Annabella cradled my body, her sobs echoing through the empty street. Her tears fell onto my face, her fingers gripping my lifeless hand as if she could will me back to life. It was the kind of grief that hollowed out a person, left them broken beyond repair.

I was still there, though not in any way that mattered. I couldn't touch her, couldn't speak to her, couldn't ease her suffering. All I could do was watch as her world collapsed around her.

The days that followed were unbearable. Annabella became a shadow of herself, lost in her grief. The light that had once returned to her eyes, the spark that had drawn me to her, was gone. In its place was a void, a hollow reflection of the pain she had carried with her for so long. Only now, it was magnified by the weight of this new loss, a grief that she hadn't known how to prepare for.

She stopped eating. Stopped sleeping. Stopped living. Luca's cries for her went unanswered. I watched him tug at her dress, begging for her attention, but she didn't see him. She was there, physically present, but her spirit was gone, buried beneath the crushing weight of sorrow. It was as if the love we had built, the life we had fought so hard to create, had been snuffed out in an instant, and nothing could bring her back from the edge.

The darkness consumed her slowly, piece by piece. I could see it happening, could feel the emptiness creeping in as she withdrew from the world. I wanted so desperately to reach out to her, to tell her that I was still there, that she wasn't alone. But I couldn't. I was powerless, bound to this invisible existence, forced to watch the love of my life fade into the same shadows that had once haunted her.

In the end, it wasn't the sickness that took her, though that was the cause written on the doctor's note. No, it was her broken heart that killed her. She had given up long before her body did. I watched her slip away, just as I had watched her struggle to hold on after I was gone. And when she finally left this world, I was still there – watching, waiting, unable to move on, because my purpose, my reason for staying, was no longer tethered to the living.

But Luca... Luca was still there. And though I couldn't reach him either, I knew my fight wasn't over yet.

I was left to witness the aftermath. Luca, so young, had to navigate a world without parents. I saw the confusion in his eyes, the way he would look around for me, for her, as if we might walk through the door at any moment. He grew up with a hole in his heart, one that no amount of love from others could fill. But he didn't let it break him.

Luca's journey was not an easy one. He fought through the pain, the loneliness, and the confusion. I watched as he struggled in school, his anger bubbling beneath the surface. He never had anyone to guide him through the grief, to help him understand why life had been so cruel to him. But despite all of it, he persevered. He channelled his pain into something constructive. He became successful – not just in his career, but as a person. He grew into a man who understood the value of life, the importance of love, and the resilience of the human spirit.

Watching him grow, I learned more about myself than I had in any lifetime before. I saw the strength that came from enduring the worst of what life could throw at you, and still finding a way to rise above it. Luca became a reflection of everything I had ever hoped to be – strong, kind, and full of love, despite the pain he had endured.

I saw his children born, watched them laugh and play, saw the love he poured into them, determined not to let them grow up with the same emptiness he had known. And as the years passed, I watched his grandchildren come into the world.

…a sanctuary from the storms that had once torn us apart, and for as long as we could hold onto it, we would.

Annabella and I were bound by a love that had been tested by the deepest darkness, forged in the fires of our broken pasts. And together, we had found a peace that defied explanation, something precious and rare, like a gift given only once in a lifetime.

But life, as it always does, had other plans. The days of simple joy, the warmth of laughter and love shared around our table, could not last forever. There came a night when fate came to claim its due, and I was thrust back into the darkness I thought I had left behind. I had gone out to help someone in need, someone who seemed lost and desperate – perhaps because I saw a glimpse of my old self in his eyes. But in that moment of kindness, I paid the ultimate price.

As I lay there, the pain searing through me, I thought of Annabella and Luca, of all the things I had yet to say, the future we had planned but would now never see. I thought of her smile, the way she held our son with such tenderness, as if her love alone could shield him from the world. I thought of all the moments I had taken for granted, all the words left unsaid, and the agony of knowing I would never hold them again. And in that final breath, I prayed – not for myself, but for them, for the strength to endure the pain that I could no longer bear.

Even in death, I couldn't leave them. I remained, as a presence, as a silent witness to their lives, watching over them from a distance, aching to comfort them yet helpless to reach out. I watched Annabella struggle, the light in her dimming as grief consumed her, as the weight of our love and our loss became too heavy to carry alone. I watched her break in ways that shattered my spirit, her once-strong heart collapsing under the strain of a love she could no longer hold.

And Luca – our precious son – he grew up carrying the legacy of a father he barely remembered. He faced the world with a strength that echoed his mother's resilience, but I saw the pain that lingered beneath his brave facade, the longing for a family that had been torn from him too soon. Despite the odds, despite the scars of a life marked by loss, he rose above the shadows, forging his own path, creating a legacy that would endure long after he was gone. I watched with pride as he became the man I could only hope to be, and his children, my grandchildren, carried pieces of us within them, fragments of our love that time could not erase.

In the end, I came to understand that love is not bound by life or death. It endures, passed down through the generations, woven into the lives of those we leave behind. And though I could no longer hold Annabella or cradle Luca in my arms, I was with them – always – my spirit bound to them by the love we shared. It was a love that transcended time, a love that even death could not sever, and as I watched my family grow and flourish,

I knew that my sacrifice had not been in vain. The pain, the heartbreak, the journey we had endured together – it had all been for something greater, something eternal.

In the silence of my afterlife, I found peace. Because in loving Annabella, in raising Luca, I had learned the truest meaning of love – that it is not something to possess, but something to give, something to leave behind, as a light for those who come after us. And though my body was gone, though my voice could no longer reach them, my love would remain, like a whispered promise carried on the wind – a quiet assurance that no matter where they went, they would never walk alone.

Chapter 7

THE SACRIFICE OF EVIL

Nothingness fell over me like a shiver spreading with spikes, sharp and sudden. A cold, bitter wave of fear crept up my spine, the kind of dread that sinks its teeth into your bones and won't let go. I felt it before I saw it – this unbearable emptiness, as though all warmth had been sucked from the world. The edges of everything blurred, as if reality itself were fraying, and I was standing on the precipice of oblivion.

Then it hit me – a scent, sharp and metallic, not of blood, but something more primal. Desperation. Panic. A choking, suffocating feeling that squeezed my chest like a vice, draining the last flickers of humanity from my soul. I was alone in the void, teetering between holding on and letting go.

I clung to the last speck of light – my only tether to what I had once been. But it was slipping away, and with it, the love I had known, the peace I had once believed in. That last speck grew dimmer until all that was left was darkness, and in that darkness, the anguish that had defined my existence was erased, replaced by something far more sinister. It wasn't grief anymore – it was loathing.

Pure, undiluted hatred coursed through me like venom, seeping into every crack of my fractured soul. The pain I had endured, the losses that had once torn me apart, now became fuel for the fire burning within me. I felt it consume me, replacing the warmth I had lost with a cold, calculating fury. I wasn't just angry – I was hungry. Hungry for vengeance, for retribution. I had been wronged, and the world would pay for it.

I stood there, bloodied, trembling with a sick kind of exhilaration, the aftermath of something I couldn't yet comprehend. I had struck someone down – felt the life drain from their body as my rage manifested in violent action. But who had I killed?

Slowly, my vision cleared, and I looked down. What I saw made my stomach lurch. The face before me wasn't the face of an enemy. It wasn't the face of a stranger.

It was mine.

I staggered back, the shock of recognition crashing into me like a tidal wave. My breath hitched, coming in short, gasping bursts as I struggled to process what I was seeing. The man lying at my feet, the one whose blood stained my hands, was me. His face – my face – twisted in agony, eyes wide and glassy, reflecting the disbelief I felt. My skin crawled, as though my own flesh recoiled at the sight. This couldn't be real.

For a brief, agonizing moment, memories surfaced, shimmering at the edge of my consciousness like mirages. Fractured, haunting visions – glimpses of a life that felt familiar yet foreign. A life I hadn't lived but had somehow endured.

In these scattered flashes, I saw fragments of myself – not the man I'd become, but a shadow twisted by despair. A version of me who had known nothing but grief and anger, a shell of who I'd once been. This other me had lost everyone he'd ever loved, watched them wither and fade, until he was left with nothing but the empty echo of their absence. I felt the bitterness seeping through the memories like poison, corrupting everything good, every shred of love I'd once held dear.

That version of me had turned away from the light, embracing only the dark. In his despair, he'd sought revenge – not just against the world, but against me, the man who had somehow found peace amidst the ruin. In a twisted way, I understood his resentment. How dare I find love, create a family, find hope, when he had known only torment? How dare I feel joy when he had been left in anguish?

The memory surged forward like a crashing wave, and I saw myself – this broken, embittered self – following me, tracking me through the streets, watching and waiting with a patient, deadly focus. And then, one night, as I turned my back to help someone, his knife found its mark.

I had killed the man I had once been.

The truth of it hit me like a punch to the gut. My stomach twisted, and I felt bile rise in my throat. This wasn't just a murder – it was a curse, a relentless cycle of suffering and rage that I had been bound to, chasing my own shadow across lifetimes. I was my own enemy, driven by a hatred so deep, so consuming, that it had turned me against myself.

In that moment, I felt my legs weaken, my hands trembling as they fell to my sides, stained with blood that felt both mine and not mine. I was crumbling, the weight of my actions pressing down on me, suffocating me. I dropped to my knees beside the lifeless body, reaching out as if to confirm that this was real – that I had truly done this. My fingers brushed the cold, unyielding flesh, and a shudder ran through me, the final nail in the coffin of my disbelief.

The loathing that had once filled me now turned inward, twisting like a knife in my chest. How could I have done this? How could I have become the very thing I had once despised? The agony of it clawed at me, tearing at the last fragments of humanity I clung to. I had sacrificed everything good in me, every drop of kindness, every flicker of hope, for the sake of vengeance. And now, I was left with nothing.

But even as the horror of my actions settled in, there was a twisted satisfaction lurking beneath the guilt. A part of me – a dark, monstrous part – felt a perverse pride in what I had done. I had taken control, shaped my own destiny, even if that control had led to my destruction. I was the villain in my own story, and for a brief, sickening moment, I revelled in it.

Then, as the blood cooled on my hands, that pride evaporated, leaving me hollow. I had lost the very last remnants of my soul, sacrificed my own humanity on the altar of vengeance. What was left now? The darkness that had filled me was gone, replaced by a terrifying emptiness – a gaping void where my anger had once been.

I was adrift, lost in a chasm of my own making, with no hope of redemption, no chance of breaking free from the torment I'd inflicted on myself.

Yet, as I knelt there in the silence, a question lingered in the shadows of my mind, faint but insistent.

Was this truly the end?

Had I doomed myself to an endless cycle, or was there a path – no matter how dim – that could lead me out of this abyss? Could I find a way to atone for what I'd done, or was my soul too shattered, too corrupted to ever be whole again?

I closed my eyes, breathing in the scent of blood and sorrow, and for the first time, I began to confront the darkness within me, not with loathing, but with a fragile, painful acceptance. I could not undo what I had done, but perhaps I could understand it. Perhaps, if I could piece together the fragments of my broken soul, there would be something left worth saving.

And so, in the silence, I began a new meditation – an introspective descent into my own darkness, seeking the origins of my rage, the roots of my suffering. Why had I been condemned to this path? What lesson was hidden in this ceaseless agony, this relentless cycle of pain?

The answers eluded me, slipping through my grasp like wisps of smoke, but I clung to the question. It was all I had left, the only light in the vast darkness.

Why must I endure this?

As I knelt there, surrounded by the echoes of my own despair, I realized that the answer would not come easily. It would require a sacrifice far greater than any I had known – a sacrifice not of blood, but of self. A surrender not to vengeance, but to understanding. To forgiveness.

And so I lingered, wrestling with the emptiness, with the flickering hope that perhaps, even in the depths of my darkness, there was a way forward.

Chapter 8

THE HUNTER WITHIN

The city stretched out before me like a maze of regrets, shadows clinging to every street and alley, each one a reflection of something I wished I could forget. I moved with purpose, my footsteps echoing against the cold stone, but beneath it all, I knew the truth: I wasn't just hunting some ghostly presence lurking in the dark. I was hunting myself.

It felt strange to think of myself as two people – a fractured reflection, a man splintered by time and sorrow. The part of me that moved with a detective's logic was sharp, methodical, piecing together clues with an almost detached sense of duty. Yet, as I moved deeper into the city's underbelly, I could feel another presence – a darker half that had once walked these very streets, leaving a trail of broken souls and blood. I was here to confront that part of myself, the one I had tried to forget.

I couldn't ignore the pull, the faint but familiar echoes that whispered to me from the past. In this life, I had sworn to bring justice, to search out the truth –

but in a previous life, I had been driven to the edge, consumed by vengeance, until I became the very thing I despised. Now, I was tracking that version of me, piecing together fragments of memories, reliving sins I barely understood but knew, deep down, were mine.

The air grew colder as I approached a desolate alley, the walls closing in like a silent witness to everything that had happened here. My hand brushed against the rough stone, feeling an almost electric charge. The detective in me, the part that sought answers, catalogued every detail – the scrape of a blade against stone, the faint smear of blood against the bricks. I knew these places because I had been here before. I was retracing steps I'd taken in another life, and every step I took seemed to close the distance between who I was and who I had been.

Clues appeared as if waiting for me – a broken weapon, stained and forgotten, lying near a hidden door; a torn note, scrawled in my own handwriting, smeared and weathered by time. Each discovery brought a fresh wave of unease. I could feel the anger, the bitterness I had once carried – alive, breathing, a part of me that refused to die.

In those moments, I could feel my identity slipping, as though I were dissolving into the shadows around me. The detective's calm resolve, that part of me that wanted to believe in redemption, clashed violently with the darker impulses clawing at the edges of my mind. I wasn't simply tracing the path of a killer; I was unravelling the deepest scars of my own soul, a wound that had never truly healed.

At last, I found myself drawn to an abandoned building, a hollow shell hidden within the heart of the city. I stepped inside, and the air grew thick with tension. In the dim light, I saw him – or rather, saw myself. It was like staring into a broken mirror. There, in the flickering shadows, stood the version of me that had long since become a monster, eyes hollow, filled with rage and pain.

I steadied myself, my voice cutting through the silence. "Why?" I asked, barely recognizing the tremor in my own voice. "Why did you become this?"

The other me – the murderer – laughed, a low, fractured sound that echoed through the empty hall. "You already know, don't you? I am you. You made me." His voice was bitter, sharp, filled with a hatred that was as much directed at me as at the world itself. "Every time you lost someone, every time you watched the people you loved slip away – those were the things that gave me life. You couldn't bear the pain, so you gave it to me."

I felt my fists clench, anger and shame boiling within me. He was right, in a way. I had created this part of myself, allowing anger to fester until it twisted into something monstrous. "I wanted to survive," I whispered, more to myself than to him. "But not like this. Not like you."

The darker part of me — the murderer — stared back, unflinching. "And yet, here we are. You think you can just erase me? Bury the part of you that kept you alive? You think redemption comes without facing your own sins?"

Suddenly, he turned and bolted into the darkness, disappearing into the shadows, and instinct took over. I chased him, heart pounding, adrenaline surging as I pushed through corridors and down stairways, my breath ragged, my mind torn between anger and fear. Every step felt like I was plunging deeper into myself, descending into memories I had tried to lock away.

I caught glimpses of him — a fleeting shadow around a corner, a silhouette slipping down another hallway. He was always just out of reach, taunting me, pulling me further into the labyrinth of my own mind. It was maddening, this chase through the corridors of my soul, as if the shadows themselves were conspiring to keep us apart. I wasn't just chasing him; I was chasing every mistake, every act of vengeance, every twisted choice that had led me to this moment.

As I gained on him, I felt something shifting inside me — a terrible, wrenching understanding that the line between us was thinner than I'd wanted to believe. I wasn't just trying to stop him; I was trying to destroy a part of myself that I could no longer bear to live with.

Finally, I cornered him in a dimly lit room, the air thick with tension, charged with an anger that seemed to pulse from both of us. We stood there, staring at each other, breathing heavily, as if waiting for the other to break. For a moment, the detective in me – the part that still believed in forgiveness – faltered, replaced by a visceral rage.

He looked at me, and for the first time, I saw a flicker of sadness in his eyes. "What will you do without me?" he whispered, almost gently. "I was the one who carried the weight. I bore the grief when you couldn't. I kept us alive."

"But at what cost?" My voice was raw, filled with the agony of years of regret. "You kept us alive, but you killed everything good in me. You turned me into this."

He smirked, though it was a broken, weary smile. "So go ahead. Kill me. Kill yourself."

And in that moment, I knew what I had to do. I raised my hand, not with anger, but with acceptance. I wasn't erasing him – I was taking him back, reclaiming the broken parts of myself that had been lost to rage and sorrow. I wasn't going to destroy him. I was going to understand him, and in doing so, let him become a part of me once more.

When the deed was done, I felt an overwhelming stillness settle over me, a peace I hadn't known in lifetimes. The murderer was gone, not in a violent, final blow, but in a quiet acceptance. I had looked into the darkness and found my own reflection staring back, fractured and bruised, but, finally, whole.

As I stepped out of the building, the world seemed lighter, the shadows less oppressive. I had walked through my own darkness, faced the sins I had tried to bury, and found the strength to carry them without letting them consume me.

I am both the hunter and the hunted, the sinner and the saint. The journey isn't over; the road ahead remains shrouded in mystery. But for the first time, I feel a sense of calm, a flicker of hope. I know now that I can walk forward, not weighed down by the past, but with a heart that has faced the worst of itself and survived.

And as I continue on this path, I know that, somehow, I am no longer alone.

Chapter 9

REDEMPTION

The cold, suffocating darkness that had once engulfed me began to give way, slowly, painfully, to something unfamiliar – a faint glimmer of hope. It was distant, a tiny spark in the ocean of despair, but it was there. It pulsed gently, inviting me to reach for it, to pull myself from the abyss I had created.

For so long, I had allowed myself to be consumed by the shadows. My journey had taken me through love, loss, and even the depths of my own evil. I had stood over my own body, a murderer of my own existence, entangled in the cycle of suffering. And now, as I stood at the precipice of my darkest hour, I realized that the only way out was not through vengeance or despair but through forgiveness.

But forgiveness, I learned, was not something that could be given lightly. It was not a single moment of release. It was a process, a painstaking climb out of the abyss, where every step felt like it could be your last, and every thought threatened to pull you back into the void.

I had to forgive myself.

I had to face the fact that in one life, I had chosen darkness over light, and in doing so, I had caused immeasurable pain – to myself, to others. But it was not just about that one life. The chain of choices I had made, life after life, had led me to this very moment. And as I stood there, teetering between the person I had become and the person I still had the potential to be, I knew that I could not move forward until I had truly faced the man I had been.

It was then that the light grew brighter, and I found myself standing in a place unlike any I had ever seen. It was not heaven, nor was it hell. It was a vast, open space, where time had no meaning, and everything – every moment of my existence – was laid bare before me. It was as if my soul had been peeled back, layer by layer, exposing the raw, unhealed wounds I had carried through lifetimes.

And there, standing before me, was the man I had once been – the man who had killed me, the man who had chosen hatred and loathing over love and compassion. His eyes were hollow, his face twisted with pain, but he was still me. He was a version of myself that I could no longer deny.

We stood there, face to face, neither of us speaking. Words seemed unnecessary in that moment. The weight of all our choices hung between us like a veil, separating us yet binding us together.

I wanted to hate him. I wanted to scream at him, to ask him why he had done what he had done. But as I looked into his eyes, I realized that I already knew the answer. He had been lost, just as I had been. He had been searching for meaning in a world that had stripped him of everything he held dear. And in his desperation, he had chosen the path that seemed easiest — the path of destruction.

But now, standing in this place of timeless reflection, I saw him not as an enemy, but as a part of myself that needed to be healed. He was the embodiment of my own pain, my own grief, my own inability to let go of the past. And if I was to be redeemed, if I was to move forward, I had to find a way to embrace him, not as a villain, but as a wounded soul in need of compassion.

I reached out, my hand trembling, and for a moment, he hesitated. But then, slowly, he lifted his own hand to meet mine. When our fingers touched, a wave of emotion crashed over me — grief, anger, regret, love — all at once. It was overwhelming, and I felt as though I might be swallowed by it.

But then, something miraculous happened. The pain that had once threatened to destroy me began to shift. It was still there, still raw and real, but it was no longer all-consuming. I felt it soften, as if the act of acknowledging it, of facing it head-on, had robbed it of its power over me.

I looked into his eyes once more, and this time, I saw not a monster, but a reflection of myself. And in that reflection, I found forgiveness. Not just for him, but for me. For all the lives I had lived, for all the mistakes I had made, for all the pain I had caused — both to myself and to others.

"I forgive you," I whispered, though the words seemed to echo through the infinite space around us.

And in that moment, the light grew brighter, enveloping us both in its warmth. The darkness that had clung to me for so long began to dissolve, replaced by a sense of peace I had never known. It was not the absence of pain, but the acceptance of it. It was the understanding that to be human was to carry both joy and sorrow, love and loss, light and dark.

As the light consumed us, I felt myself begin to change. I was no longer divided, no longer torn between the person I had been and the person I wanted to become. I was whole, for the first time in lifetimes. And with that wholeness came the knowledge that my journey was far from over.

There would be more lives to live, more lessons to learn, more love to give. But for now, in this moment, I was at peace. I had found redemption — not in erasing the past, but in embracing it, in forgiving myself, in understanding that even in my darkest hour, I had the capacity for light.

And as I moved forward, I knew that the man I had once been would always be a part of me. But he no longer controlled me. He was a chapter in my story, not the end of it.

I stepped into the light, ready to begin again.

Chapter 10

THE LIGHT OF FIRST BREATH

I came into the world without a past or future – only this single moment, fragile and beautiful. There was a warmth that cradled me, surrounding me in a soft cocoon, a world where everything was gentle and kind. I opened my eyes, and though the world was blurry, I could feel it even more clearly than I could see. Love enveloped me, brighter than the light I had stepped into, a radiant warmth that I understood without words. I was held.

I was only hours old, my senses awakened to the world, each moment infinite, each breath a new discovery. I felt strong hands supporting me, steady and protective, and soft whispers that I didn't understand, but I knew were meant only for me. I recognized voices as if I had known them forever – a deep, calming tone that vibrated like a steady heartbeat and a lighter, softer voice that rose and fell like a lullaby.

My world was made of those sounds, those touches, the warmth of skin against mine. I felt the brush of a hand on my cheek, the gentle rhythm of a heartbeat as

I was nestled close, the steady breaths of the ones who held me with a love so intense that it felt like an endless embrace. In those moments, I knew only peace, only the fullness of being loved without condition, without limits.

I didn't know how long I would stay, but I felt no fear. I didn't know the name for sorrow, nor did I know the sting of loss. I just was. And that was enough. Every second stretched on like an eternity, each one filled with all that mattered. I felt the love in the way they held me as if they were trying to pour their entire souls into that embrace. And I gave them everything in return, though I had no words for it — just a quiet presence, a sense of pure, mutual belonging.

Their faces were the first images my eyes had ever seen. My mother's face was soft and warm, her eyes filled with light as she looked down at me, her lips forming a gentle smile. I recognized her even though we had only just met, and I loved her with all that I was, with a love that didn't need time to grow. I saw my father, his face strong yet softened with an expression I couldn't name but knew instinctively. I knew I was safe with them. I knew that I was theirs, and they were mine.

I drifted in and out, sometimes closing my eyes, sinking back into that cocoon of warmth and light, only to open them and find them both still there, still looking at me as if nothing else existed. There was no rush, no sense that time was slipping away. All that mattered was that I was here, that they were here, and that love filled every breath, every heartbeat, every gentle touch.

As I grew tired, I felt their love wrapping around me like a blanket, filling me until I was complete, a vessel overflowing with their joy, their hopes, their dreams. They whispered words I couldn't understand, but I felt the meaning as clearly as if it were written into my very soul. I was loved. I was wanted. I was cherished.

There was no pain here, no hardship, no weight of the world pressing down. There was only this moment, this pure, unbreakable bond. I knew, even without words, that my time was short. I could feel it as surely as I felt their love. But that didn't matter, because I was whole. I had known love without suffering, joy without fear. And though my journey was brief, I felt as though I had lived a lifetime in those precious hours, because I had experienced everything that truly mattered.

I took a deep breath, my last gift to this world, and in that breath, I felt a peace I had never known before. I knew, in the deepest part of myself, that I would return to the light. That I would find them again, somewhere, somehow. Because love like this was eternal; it would not end here. This love, this fleeting moment, would remain, etched into the fabric of all that was and all that would be. I was complete.

As I drifted back into the quiet space between worlds, I held onto the lingering warmth of my brief life, each memory of love still glowing within me like embers in a darkened night. It had been such a fleeting existence, so small, and yet it felt as if it had filled every part of me, leaving me somehow lighter. There had been no fear, no loss, no struggle – only pure, untainted love.

It was strange to consider: after lifetimes of searching, learning, suffering, and striving, this smallest moment had granted me what I'd been reaching for all along. And it wasn't in the triumphs of my past lives, nor in the wisdom of ages, but in the softness of a mother's touch, the pride in a father's embrace, and the safety in their arms. It was as if in my short, silent presence, I had become a vessel to remind them of their own capacity to love, without expectation or judgment.

The reflection of that life lingered in my mind, clear and still, like a pond unbroken by ripples. I understood now that love need not be weighed by time or trials. It simply was, and in that realization, I felt as if I had finally touched the essence of my soul.

For so long, I had seen love as something one earned, fought for, or suffered to obtain. I had believed that to be worthy of love, one must sacrifice, prove, or redeem themselves in some way. I had carried that belief across lifetimes, convinced that only by enduring hardship could one grasp love's true meaning. And yet, in this quiet existence, I had learned something simpler, something truer:

Love wasn't something I had to strive for. It was something I was.

This revelation settled into the deepest part of me. In the silence that followed, I felt an overwhelming peace, as if the question that had haunted me through my journey – What is my purpose? Why must I endure? – was no longer a question at all. My purpose was not in seeking answers, but in simply being.

In that brief life, I hadn't accomplished anything, hadn't changed the world, or made any sacrifices. I had simply been loved, and in that love, I had found all that I needed.

The moment felt like an invitation to let go of all the weight I'd carried. I had been a warrior, a brother, a lover, a healer, a guide – roles that had brought both meaning and suffering. Each life had shaped me, pushing me forward, as if my soul were a flame searching for something it couldn't yet name. But now, in this soft, gentle light, I realized I didn't need to push any longer.

I had found peace.

Perhaps I would return to the journey. Perhaps I would continue to search, to live, to learn. But now, I understood that whatever life held for me, the core of my existence was already whole, unbroken.

I didn't have to suffer to deserve love. I didn't need to seek pain to find meaning. I had come into the world simply to experience love as it was, for however long it lasted, and that had been enough.

As I drifted in the quiet, I felt a question rise up from within, not in words but in a feeling, a pull toward the unknown. What will come next?

I didn't know the answer. And for the first time in all my journeys, I was content not knowing. In that peace, I felt ready – ready for whatever lay ahead, knowing that whatever I faced, I would carry this love with me. It was an eternal light, something no hardship or sorrow could ever extinguish.

And so, as I prepared to step forward once more, I whispered a promise to myself, a vow carried not in words but in the essence of my being:

Whatever path I walk, I will carry this love with me. And it will be enough.

And as I drifted back into the light, I carried their love with me.

Chapter 11

THE RIVER OF TIME

Time, I began to understand, was not a straight line but a vast river, flowing in all directions at once. The lives I had lived, the lessons I had learned, weren't laid out in a simple sequence, like the orderly pages of a book. They were simultaneous, overlapping currents in an endless, rushing river. Each life, each moment, each memory, was like a drop of water caught in that flow. And I – was just one of many souls navigating its endless depths.

Standing on the riverbank, I could feel time's currents pulling me, nudging me in every direction. Some drew me backward, whispering of moments I thought I had left behind – the loves and losses, the victories and defeats of past lives. Others tugged me forward, hinting at futures still to be written, chapters not yet known. And there, amid the pull of past and future, I could feel myself – no longer just the man I had been, but all the people I might ever become.

I reached into the river, my hand grazing the surface. In that instant, countless lives rippled through my fingertips. The water felt warm and cold, as if carrying the pulse of history itself. I saw them there – my former selves, my loved ones from lifetimes past, some clear and close, others little more than shadows, blurred by the passing of ages.

The river wasn't cruel. Nor was it kind. It simply was – a relentless, impartial force, flowing without end, carrying the weight of joy and sorrow, triumph and defeat alike. It didn't mourn or celebrate; it held no judgment. It simply flowed, indifferent to the stories we told ourselves or the significance we clung to.

But I wasn't indifferent. Each life I had lived mattered to me, each soul I had touched, each heartache I had endured. They had etched themselves into me, a map of scars and memories, and even here, in the vastness of time, I could still feel their weight. I could still feel the shape of my story.

And in that moment, I understood something profound: time wasn't my enemy. It wasn't something to fight against, something to master or control. It was my teacher, guiding me through the vastness of existence, allowing me to glimpse the infinite possibilities of who I might become.

The river asked me to release my grip on certainty, to accept that not every piece of the puzzle was mine to know. It carried me forward, showing me moments of love, loss, joy, and pain, weaving them together until they became a single, unbroken thread. Time, it seemed, was not merely a sequence to navigate but an endless canvas, a flowing tapestry into which each of us – every soul that had ever been – was woven.

So, I took a step forward. I let go of my fears, my need to know what lay ahead. I released my hold on the past, on all the lives I had once known, and allowed the river to carry me. For the first time, I no longer felt separate from the current; I was a part of it, boundless, timeless, one with its flow.

As I surrendered to the river, a sense of profound peace washed over me. I realized I didn't need to see where it led, didn't need to control its direction or anticipate its turns. The river would guide me as it always had, through all my lifetimes and all my lessons, and that would be enough.

Past and future blurred, merging into one continuous stream, and I flowed with it, feeling time's presence within me – a quiet understanding that all things were connected, that nothing was ever truly lost.

For a moment, I felt the brush of familiar souls beside me, those who had shaped me across lifetimes. They were there, moving alongside me, their spirits woven with mine, as we flowed together into the mystery that lay beyond.

Somewhere in the depths of that river, I felt a whisper, a silent vow echoing within me: I would continue to learn, continue to grow, but most of all, I would carry forward the love and wisdom gathered along my journey. Every twist, every turn, every joy and sorrow would add to the river's flow, and in turn, it would shape me.

And so, I let go, releasing myself to the river, knowing that wherever it led, I would find what I was searching for.

In the end, I was not alone. The river of time carried us all, each soul a current in its depths, connected in ways we might never fully understand. But perhaps understanding wasn't necessary. Perhaps the truth was not in knowing but in feeling, in letting the river carry us, in surrendering to the journey.

As I drifted, I felt a quiet joy – a realization that, whatever the future held, I was part of something infinite, something vast and beautiful.

And that was enough.

Chapter 12

BECOMING WHOLE

The lives I had lived, the trials I had endured, the loves and losses, the joys and the anguish – each had left a mark upon me, a part of me I could not shed. And as I stood on the edge of the river of time, I finally saw the pattern. I was never meant to find perfection. I was meant to find completion. The journey wasn't about achieving an ideal existence – it was about becoming whole, woven together by the sum of my parts, my flaws, my virtues, my regrets, and my dreams.

I felt something profound shift within me, a quiet settling of pieces that had once felt scattered, distant. Emerging from the river, I felt the pull of time fall away, leaving me here in a moment that felt both infinite and fleeting. I was no longer only Tristan. I was the warrior who had fought for justice and the father who had wept for his child. I was the guide who had whispered to heroes and the sinner who had stumbled in darkness. I was the lover, the killer, the healer, the dreamer. And in that instant, I was whole.

A warmth began to rise within me. It started as a faint glow, growing steadily, spreading through me like fire and light. It filled my veins, my muscles, my very bones with something vast and ancient. This light wasn't merely mine; it was all the lives I had ever lived, all the souls I had ever loved, every connection I had made, every lesson I had learned. I felt the warmth of my wife's embrace, the laughter of my child, the tears shed by friends and foes alike. I felt the fears that had once held me and the peace that had eluded me – until now.

I began to radiate with that light, a force that seemed to rise from the core of my being and beyond. It was as though every piece of myself, every past self, every loved one, every scar and triumph, were coming together as one. I felt that I was no longer simply a man standing on the riverbank; I was becoming something more – something woven into the fabric of existence itself.

But this wasn't an end. It was only the next step. I could feel it – the pulse of life, the rhythm of creation, the heartbeat that connected all things. I was no longer just a drop in the river; I was a part of its essence, woven into its currents, its endless flow.

For so long, I'd believed the goal was to transcend, to escape this cycle of life and death, to reach a higher state of being. But now, standing here, I finally understood: there was no escape, because there was nothing to escape from. The journey itself was the answer. Every struggle, every joy, every loss was not an obstacle but a gift – a piece of the puzzle that, together, made me whole.

So, I stood there, glowing with the light of a thousand lives, and for the first time, I smiled not from relief or victory, but from the simplest, purest contentment. I was no longer searching for meaning – I *was* the meaning. I was no longer seeking purpose – I *was* the purpose. I had come to understand that to be whole meant to embrace it all, every shard of experience, every emotion. I was ready for whatever would come next.

As the light grew brighter, a gentle tug pulled at me, urging me forward. This time, I felt no fear, no doubt, no hesitation. Whatever awaited me, I was ready. I had lived, I had loved, I had lost, I had learned. And now, I was whole.

Taking a step forward, I felt the world dissolve into pure, radiant light. The river of time, the echoes of past lives, the faces of those I had known – all melted away, leaving only warmth and a profound, quiet peace.

I was becoming one with the universe, one with the source of all things. But rather than fading, I was expanding, becoming more than I had ever imagined, woven into the very fabric of existence.

In that final moment, I understood the truth that had eluded me all along: there was no end to the journey. There was no final destination. There was only the eternal flow of life, the endless dance of creation, and the infinite love that binds us all together.

I had become whole. But the journey would never end.

And that was the most beautiful truth of all.

About the Author

Gary J. Robbins is a novelist whose work draws deeply from his own journey through life's profound highs and lows. His storytelling is infused with experiences of grief, resilience, and compassion, reflecting an understanding of the human spirit that reaches beyond personal challenges. He is a listener and an observer, inspired by the connections he forges with people from all walks of life. Through shared dreams, candid conversations, and exploring the loyalties that bind us, Robbins brings authenticity and depth to his writing, inviting readers to reflect on the threads of love, loss, and redemption that run through all of us.

In his writing, Robbins strives to translate not only his life's trials and tribulations but also the quiet, enduring kindness he sees in others. His narratives are journeys that transcend the boundaries of time and space, weaving together the ethereal and the deeply personal to offer perspectives that linger with his readers long after the final page. With each story, he seeks to inspire, uplift, and remind us of the profound interconnectedness that defines our shared human experience.

www.ingramcontent.com/pod-product-compliance
Lightning Source LLC
Chambersburg PA
CBHW050804250626
47155CB00005B/2211